Grade 2
Alto Sax

CW00499421

Chester Music
part of The Music Sales Group
London/New York/Paris/Sydney/Copenhagen/Berlin/Madrid/Hong Kong/Tokyo

Published by

Chester Music
part of The Music Sales Group
14-15 Berners Street, London W1T 3LJ, UK.

Exclusive Distributors:
Music Sales Limited
Distribution Centre, Newmarket Road,
Bury St Edmunds, Suffolk IP33 3YB, UK.

Music Sales Pty Limited
Level 4, Lisgar House,
30-32 Carrington Street,
Sydney, NSW 2000 Australia.

Order No. CH84117
ISBN 978-1-78558-069-7
This book © Copyright 2015 Chester Music Limited.
All Rights Reserved.

Edited by Jenni Norey.
Arranged and engraved by Christopher Hussey.
With thanks to Sandra Gamba.

Printed in the EU.

Your Guarantee of Quality
As publishers, we strive to produce every book to the
highest commercial standards.
This book has been carefully designed to minimise awkward
page turns and to make playing from it a real pleasure.
Particular care has been given to specifying acid-free, neutral-sized paper
made from pulps which have not been elemental chlorine bleached.
This pulp is from farmed sustainable forests and was
produced with special regard for the environment.
Throughout, the printing and binding have been planned to
ensure a sturdy, attractive publication which should give years of enjoyment.
If your copy fails to meet our high standards,
please inform us and we will gladly replace it.

www.musicsales.com

Saxophone Fingering Chart

LIGATURE

MOUTHPIECE

CROOK

THUMB SUPPORT

BODY

2L
3L
1ST FINGER
1L
4L
5L
2ND FINGER
3RD FINGER
6L
7L
8L
9L

LEFT HAND

OCTAVE KEY

THUMB REST

1R

2R

3R

*4R

1ST FINGER

5R

2ND FINGER

3RD FINGER

6R

7R

RIGHT HAND

THE RING

* Not fitted on some saxophones

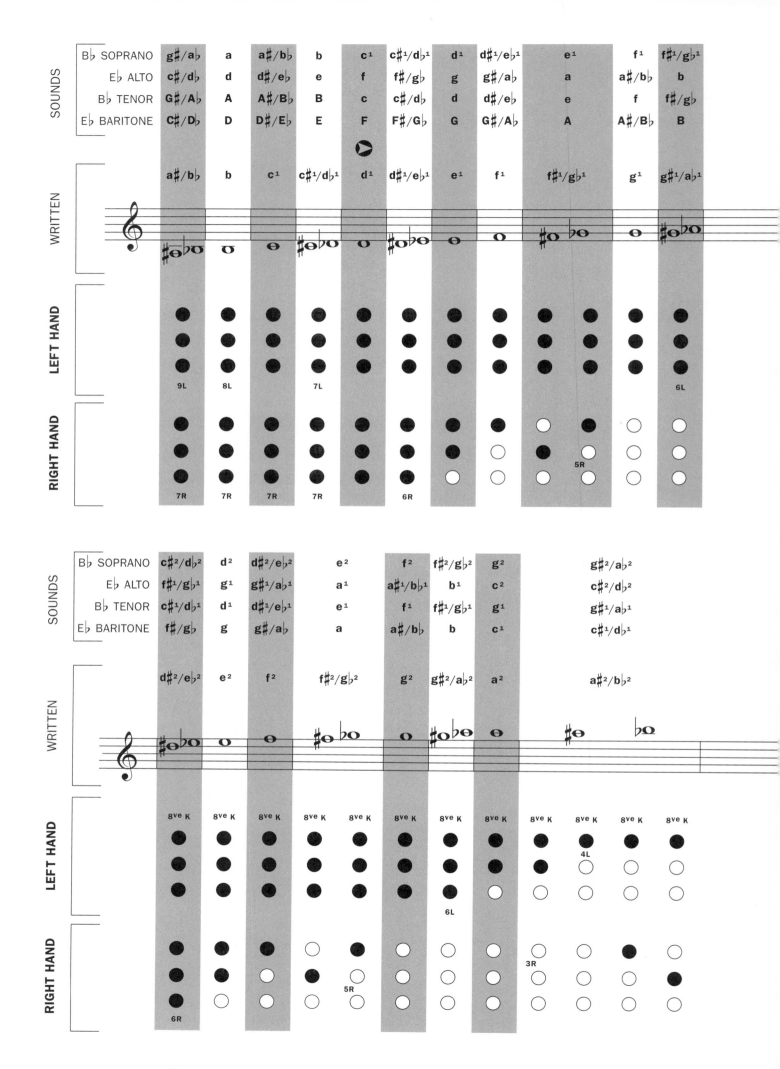

Indicates the lower limit of the best playing range

Indicates the upper limit of the best playing range

Atlas
from *The Hunger Games: Catching Fire*

Taken from the soundtrack to *The Hunger Games: Catching Fire*, part two of *The Hunger Games* trilogy, this is the first song Coldplay wrote specifically for a film. Lead singer Chris Martin is apparently a fan of the books by Suzanne Collins, on which the films are based.

Bridge Over Troubled Water
Simon & Garfunkel

This is the title track of the UK's best-selling album of the 1970s. Later on, when Paul Simon heard the appreciative applause Art Garfunkel received as lead singer, he remarked bitterly "...that's my song, man, thank you very much. I wrote that song!"

Hallelujah
Leonard Cohen

First recorded (with 15 verses!) by Leonard Cohen on his 1984 album *Various Positions*, and nominated by Q Magazine in September 2007 as the most perfect song ever, various versions of this song have featured on the soundtracks of several movies and TV shows.

He Ain't Heavy, He's My Brother
The Hollies

Released in September 1969, this song became one of the most defining and enduring tunes of the 1960s. Commonly associated with Manchester, The Hollies had a squeaky-clean image, and were famous for their rich vocal harmonies, which rivalled those of The Beach Boys.

I Have A Dream
Westlife

Originally recorded and released by ABBA in 1979, this song has been covered many times. The most famous version is the one by Westlife, released 20 years later, which reached No. 1 in the UK charts — beating the original by one place!

I Will Always Love You
Whitney Houston

Dolly Parton's breathy farewell song to her ex-singing partner Porter Wagoner was hardly typical of her early compositions but it was still a surprise when Whitney Houston covered it. Houston's mega-selling movie version, from the film *The Bodyguard*, made both of them rich.

Just Give Me A Reason
Pink

'Just Give Me A Reason' is a duet featuring Nate Ruess, lead singer of Fun, and was the third single from Pink's sixth studio album *The Truth About Love*. Even before its official release, the song charted in multiple regions due to strong digital download sales. In the USA alone, the song eventually sold two million copies through digital downloads.

Let It Go
from *Frozen*

The smash hit song from the film *Frozen*, 'Let It Go' was written by Kirsten Anderson-Lopez and her husband Robert Lopez, who was behind the music for *Avenue Q* and *The Book Of Mormon*. In 2013 *Frozen* became the highest-grossing animated film, earning a whopping $110.6 million during its opening week! 'Let It Go' is sung by Queen Elsa, who is just discovering that her magical power to control and create ice no longer has to hold her back.

Mamma Mia
ABBA

The song that two decades later lent its name to the international smash ABBA musical first came out in 1975. Apparently, ABBA manager Stig Anderson came up with the title and band members Björn Ulvaeus and Benny Andersson wrote the lyrics to fit around it.

Once Upon A Dream
from *Maleficent*

In a new angle for Disney, *Maleficent* tells the story of Sleeping Beauty from the point of view of the infamous fairy Maleficent, played by Angelina Jolie. 'Once Upon A Dream', covered for this film by Lana Del Rey, featured in Disney's original animated version of the story and was based on a waltz from Tchaikovsky's ballet *The Sleeping Beauty*.

Waterloo
ABBA

'Waterloo' is the legendary breakout song with which four strangely-dressed Swedes won *The Eurovision Song Contest* in Brighton, England, in 1974. One critic said the hook-line of 'Waterloo' stayed with you like a kick in the knee, but everyone else knew the song marked the start of something special.

What A Wonderful World
Louis Armstrong

While the boss of ABC records hated this song, Louis Armstrong loved it so much he agreed to record it for his union fee of $250. Many people now associate jazz music's greatest pioneer with this charming ballad.

What Makes You Beautiful
One Direction

The success of this song helped to propel One Direction into becoming one of the biggest pop acts around, conquering the USA at the head of a new British Invasion. At the 2012 BRIT Awards the band's success was recognised with the trophy for Best British Single, an award that was soon joined by gongs from the MTV Video Music Awards and Teen Choice Awards.

Wrecking Ball
Miley Cyrus

Miley Cyrus was arguably the most talked about pop star of 2013, with the former *Hannah Montana* singer grabbing the headlines (and lighting up social media) with her raunchy antics, videos and performances. 'Wrecking Ball' was her greatest landmark in a year full of many memorable moments with the track coming in No. 1 in the UK, Spain, Canada, Mexico and many other countries.

Yellow Submarine
The Beatles

Ringo, unusually, sings lead vocal on this track. The melange of different watery sound effects and even a brass band, shows that the Beatles were moving further and further away from a recording style that could be reproduced live by the band.

Atlas

Words & Music by Guy Berryman, Jonathan Buckland, William Champion & Christopher Martin

Pivot your back thumb onto the register key cleanly during the leaps (in bars 6, 10, 14 etc.).

There are many ties and slurs in this song—try practising these bars without them at first, as you learn the rhythms.

Don't forget the key change in bar 37—you only have to remember the F♯s in the new key.

Bridge Over Troubled Water

Words & Music by Paul Simon

Join each note by pushing the air through so that the tongued notes don't sound too detached. This is called *legato tonguing*.

Watch out for the rhythm in bar 21—make sure the B lands on the third beat of the bar.

Hallelujah

Words & Music by Leonard Cohen

As you start learning this song, count six quavers in each bar, and when you feel confident with the rhythm, start thinking in two dotted crotchet beats per bar.

Use *legato tonguing* so that each note is connected without sounding too detached.

He Ain't Heavy, He's My Brother

Words & Music by Bob Russell & Robert William Scott

The rhythm in bar 6 appears often in this song, so make sure you work this out first. Take out the ties to get the dotted rhythm before trying it as written.

Remember the F♯s in the key signature.

I Have A Dream

Words & Music by Benny Andersson & Björn Ulvaeus

Build up some air pressure ready to start the low Ds so that they don't blurt out when tongued.

Remember the F♯s in the key signature.

I Will Always Love You

Words & Music by Dolly Parton

The bars with the syncopated rhythms (for example, bars 7 and 11) are quite tricky. Count in quavers at first, as you learn the rhythms.

Remember the F♯s in the key signature.

Just Give Me A Reason

Words & Music by Alecia Moore, Jeff Bhasker & Nate Ruess

This song is fun to play as the rhythms are easy, but watch out for the B♮s.

Some of the leaps in the second section of the piece (bar 21 onwards) will need some extra practise.

Let It Go

Words & Music by Kirsten Anderson-Lopez and Robert Lopez.

Make sure you count carefully through the ties and perform the articulation as written.

Really enjoy the *forte* dynamic (marked f) for the chorus, beginning in bar 34.

Mamma Mia

Words & Music by Benny Andersson, Stig Anderson & Björn Ulvaeus

Use a light but precise tongue for the staccato in bar 29, and then contrast that with some full accents in bar 31. Watch your tone when accenting the high Cs and Bs (in bars 24 and 26)—use a belly kick instead of a hard tongue.

Remember the F♯s in the key signature.

Once Upon A Dream

Words & Music by Sammy Fain & Jack Lawrence

There are quite a few accidentals in this song, so make sure you know where they are before you play. Remember the F♯s and C♯s in the key signature. D♯ is another name for E♭.

C♯s can sound quite weak, so keep a round mouth shape and be careful not to bite down on the reed.

Waterloo

Words & Music by Benny Andersson, Stig Anderson & Björn Ulvaeus

The quavers in this song are swung so make sure the first quaver of each pair is longer than the second—'doo-bi'.

Be careful to play the correct articulation, especially where you play repeated notes after a slur, for example in bar 14.

What A Wonderful World

Words & Music by Bob Thiele & George Weiss

Count this song in six quavers per bar until you are confident with the rhythm.

Make sure you understand all the repeats before you begin!

What Makes You Beautiful

Words & Music by Savan Kotecha, Carl Falk & Rami Yacoub

Put lots of energy into the quavers so the melody has a sense of driving forwards.

You may need to practise bar 17 without the ties a few times at first, to get the rhythm right.

Wrecking Ball

Words & Music by Stephan Moccio, Sacha Skarbek, Lukasz Gottwald, Henry Russell Walter & Maureen McDonald

Make sure your fingers move cleanly during the leaps at the beginning of the song. Special attention should be paid to your back thumb when moving on and off the register key—remember to pivot.

The triplets in bar 29 are to be played over two crotchet beats.

Yellow Submarine

Words & Music by John Lennon & Paul McCartney

The quavers in this song are swung so make sure the first quaver of each pair is longer than the second—'doo-bi'.

123456789

COLLECT THE SERIES
Graded Alto Saxophone Pieces
15 Popular Practice Pieces

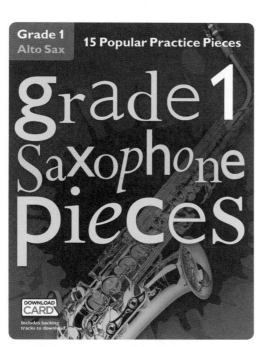

Grade 1 Alto Saxophone Pieces
CH84106

Grade 2 Alto Saxophone Pieces
CH84117

Grade 3 Alto Saxophone Pieces
CH84128

Available from all good music shops

or, in case of difficulty contact:
Music Sales Limited, Newmarket Road, Bury St Edmunds, Suffolk, IP33 3YB, UK.
music@musicsales.co.uk

HOW TO DOWNLOAD YOUR MUSIC TRACKS

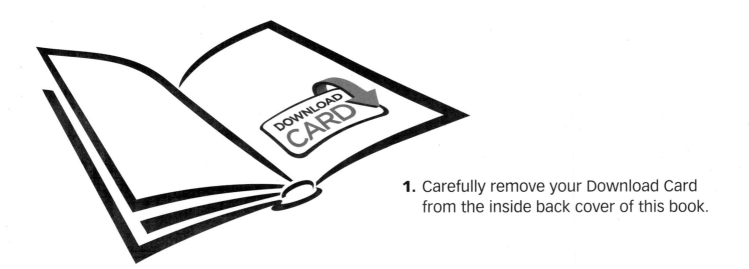

1. Carefully remove your Download Card from the inside back cover of this book.

TO REDEEM THIS CARD VISIT
www.musicsalesdownloads.com
ENTER ACCESS CODE:

`XXXXXXXXX`

Download Cards are powered by Dropcards.
User must accept terms at dropcards.com/terms
which are adopted by The Music Sales Group.
Not redeemable for cash. Void where prohibited or restricted by law.

DCARD1006478

2. On the back of the card is your unique access code. Enter this at www.musicsalesdownloads.com

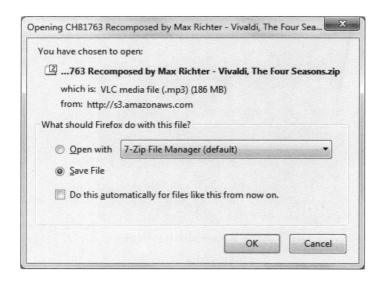

Opening CH81763 Recomposed by Max Richter - Vivaldi, The Four Sea...

You have chosen to open:

  ...763 Recomposed by Max Richter - Vivaldi, The Four Seasons.zip

  which is: VLC media file (.mp3) (186 MB)
  from: http://s3.amazonaws.com

What should Firefox do with this file?

  ○ Open with   7-Zip File Manager (default)
  ● Save File
  ☐ Do this automatically for files like this from now on.

  OK   Cancel

3. Follow the instructions to save your files to your computer*. That's it!

*Appearance of download manager will vary depending upon operating system and web browser.
In case of difficulty when downloading files, please contact dropcards.com/help
Card missing? Please contact music@musicsales.co.uk